Where'd My Jo Go?

Written by JILL ESBAUM
and Illustrated by SCOTT BRUNDAGE

PUBLISHED BY SLEEPING BEAR PRESS

For my grandkiddos, and for our family's sweet doggy pals,
Brodie, Bridget, and Sunny
—Jill

For Miga
—Scott

Text Copyright © 2020 Jill Esbaum
Illustration Copyright © 2020 Scott Brundage
Design © 2020 Sleeping Bear Press

Sleeping Bear Press™

2395 South Huron Parkway, Suite 200,
Ann Arbor, MI 48104
www.sleepingbearpress.com
© Sleeping Bear Press

Printed and bound in the United States.
10 9 8 7 6 5 4 3 2 1

Library of Congress Cataloging-in-Publication Data
Names: Esbaum, Jill, author. | Brundage, Scott, illustrator.
Title: Where'd my Jo go? / written by Jill Esbaum ; illustrated by Scott Brundage.
Other titles: Where did my Jo go?
Description: Ann Arbor, MI : Sleeping Bear Press, [2020] | Audience: Ages
4-8. | Summary: When Big Al the little dog gets separated from his
trucker friend, Jo, at a roadside rest area, he patiently waits, resisting
the attention of other drivers, knowing that Jo will return and find him.
Identifiers: LCCN 2019036851 | ISBN 9781534110441 (hardcover)
Subjects: CYAC: Stories in rhyme. | Dogs—Fiction. | Truck
drivers—Fiction. | Lost and found possessions—Fiction.
Classification: LCC PZ8.3.E818 Whe 2020 | DDC [E]—dc23
LC record available at https://lccn.loc.gov/2019036851

Always together,
wherever they go.

Jo and Big Al,
Big Al and Jo.

Adjust a mirror, set the map.
Pull the belt across my lap.

Let another trucker pass.
Shift the gears, give 'er gas.

Dodge a herd of stompy feet.

Sneak a lick of someone's treat.

Chase a wrapper.

Dig in dirt.

Give a tree a
little squirt.

Roll in flowers.

"No-no-NO!"

Time for me to
go-
go-
go!

Searching up and down the line.

Lots of trucks, but where is mine?

It's gone!
The truck's gone!
Holy cow!

Where'd my Jo go, anyhow?

Could I find her? Should I—

No!

SIT. STAY. Wait for Jo.

who shares her lunch,

who guards the truck,

whose head she
rub-rub-rubs for luck.

Who helps her pack
her duffel bag,

plays tug-of-war

and fetch

and tag.

A too-loud kid yells,
"HIYA, PUP!"

She tries to kiss me!
I back up.

She chases me!

"COME HOME WITH US!"

I run around a shiny bus.

I sniff somebody's picnic trash.
Wander through their campfire ash.
Wonder where my Jo could be.

Oh, Jo. Please, Jo, remember me.

No trucks. No people. Spooky. Late.
Chase a june bug.

Shiver. Wait.

A car pulls in.
A kid gets out.

"Hey, look!
A dog! Alone!"
he shouts.

Kid wants to play.
He throws a stick.

Can. Not. Resist.

I fetch it, quick.

He thinks I'm lost,
this kid, this Zack.
He doesn't know Jo's coming back.

Zack says, **"Pleeease, Dad?**

It isn't right to leave him here alone at night."

I should not, cannot, will not go.

But ohhh, I like Zack. Hurry, Jo.

Zack hugs me tight. I lick his chin, and . . .

hear another truck pull in.

I have to look.
Could it be true?
Oh, Jo. Please, Jo,
could that be—

onk-onk!
onk-onnnnnnnnk!

Yip-yip!

Bye, Zack! I have to go!

I knew she'd come!
It's her!

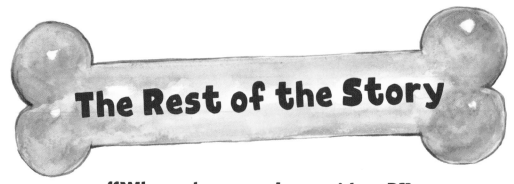

The Rest of the Story

"Where do you get your ideas?"

Authors are often asked that question. I usually reply, "Ideas are everywhere!"–even though I know that isn't a very satisfying answer. But because writers are good at keeping our minds and hearts open, and because we tend to have imaginations that run wild when unleashed, it's sometimes difficult to pinpoint exactly *what* it was we saw, heard, or felt that sparked a story idea.

This book is different, though, because I know exactly where I got the idea for Big Al's tale: I read a newspaper story about a long-distance trucker who, hours after stopping at a rest area, discovered that his beloved pal was missing.

In real life, the trucker couldn't turn around. If he didn't deliver his goods, he'd lose his job!

In real life, he called the police for help. But somebody lost the message.

In real life, the dog waited patiently for *two whole days* before he was found.

The story had a happy-yappy ending. Whew! Still . . . I couldn't stop thinking about that poor little dog and how confused he must have felt when he trotted back to his truck and–*Oh no! It's gone!*

Can you *imagine*?!

With that little dog stuck in my head, I sure could. So I wrote part of the story from his point of view. Lost and bewildered, worried yet never doubting that his best friend would come back for him if only he stayed put.

Give it a try. Pick a person (or animal!) from a story you like who *isn't* the main character. Tell the story from that new point of view. Just put yourself into that character's head, heart, and feelings, then jump inside the story and let your imagination off the leash! *Yip-yip!*

–Jill Esbaum